To Grandad,

Happy GranDaD's Day!

You've always been our favorite......

lots of love

Holly & Ruby

x x x

Designed by Andrea Newton
Language consultant: Betty Root

This is a Parragon book
This edition published in 2003
Parragon, Queen Street House, 4 Queen Street,
BATH BA1 1HE, UK
Copyright © Parragon 2001

ISBN 1-40540-454-X
Printed in Singapore

My Grandpa is Great

Written by Gaby Goldsack

Illustrated by Sara Walker

p

My grandpa is **great**. He always has lots of time for me, even when he's busy.

I always look forward to going to stay with him for the weekend.

Grandpa is a lot like me.
He enjoys getting lovely and dirty.

I just wish Grandma
felt the same way.

Grandpa is a **brilliant** gardener.
His pumpkins are the biggest I've ever seen.

Well, that was until I saw even bigger ones at the village show. Luckily, Grandpa doesn't mind.

He's a great sport!

My grandpa is a **great** fisherman.

But he always forgets the size
of the fish that he caught.
Luckily, I'm there to remind him!

Grandpa knows all about the countryside.
He knows the names of every bird and flower.

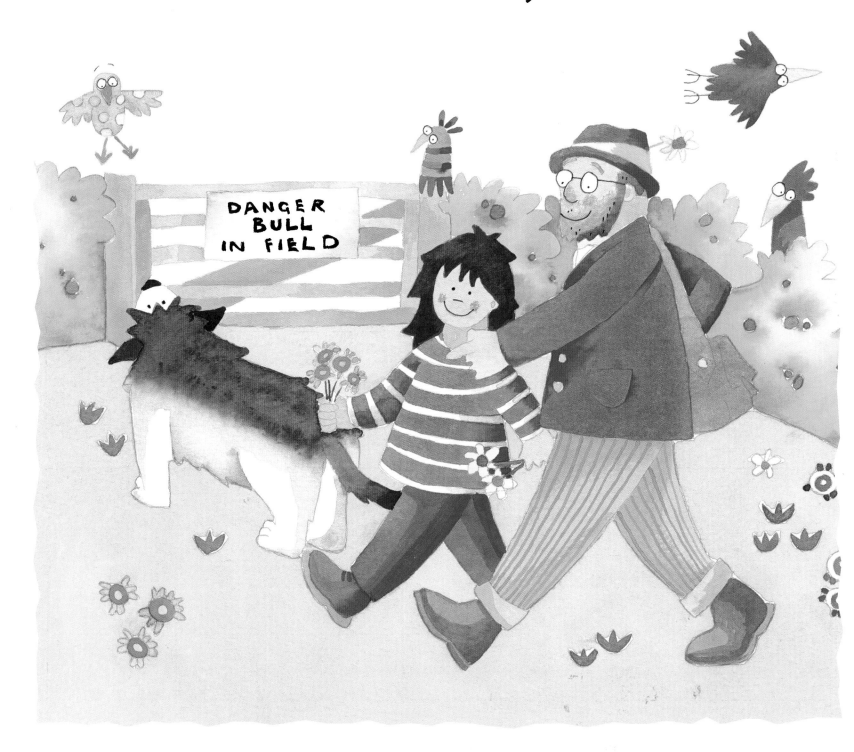

He even knows the quickest way to get away from danger! It's amazing how fast he can run.

Grandpa is a **fantastic** dancer.

I love dancing with him, but sometimes it makes me feel a bit dizzy. I don't know where he gets his energy.

Grandpa has lots of cool toys.

Sometimes he even lets me play with them!

Grandpa is very handy in the house.
I can't wait to show Grandma
what he's done to the kitchen!

PIZZA

My grandpa is a **brilliant** cook, too.
He says that when I grow up he'll tell me the
secret of making a really good pizza.

Sometimes Grandpa takes me to watch a match.

He's the star of the team.

Grandpa tells me all kinds of **amazing** stories. It's hard to believe that he used to be a pirate.

I wish I could have seen his
big, red pirate ship.

Sometimes, if I'm really lucky,
Grandpa lets me sleep in his tent.

When he's with me, I'm never afraid.

When it's time to go home,
I wave goodbye to Grandpa.

I expect he's really busy when I'm not there to help. My grandpa is so kind and funny. I love going to Grandpa's because ...

my grandpa is G-R-E-A-T!